I Can Read!

Adventures of

Biscuit

Five Stories About
Everyone's Favorite Puppy

by Alyssa Satin Capucilli • pictures by Pat Schories

Sandy Creek

Sandy Creek
387 Park Avenue South
New York, NY 10016

ISBN-13: 978-0-7607-7108-2

Manufactured in China

Manufactured 04/2012

Lot 12 13 SCP 20 19 18 17 16 15 14 13 12

Contents

Biscuit

*For Laura and Peter who wait patiently
for a Biscuit of their very own*
–A. S. C.

For Tess
–P. S.

This is Biscuit.

Biscuit is small.

Biscuit is yellow.

Time for bed, Biscuit!

Woof, woof!

Biscuit wants to play.

Time for bed, Biscuit!

Woof, woof!

Biscuit wants a snack.

Time for bed, Biscuit!

Woof, woof!

Biscuit wants a drink.

Time for bed, Biscuit!

Woof, woof!

Biscuit wants to hear a story.

Time for bed, Biscuit!

Woof, woof!

Biscuit wants his blanket.

Time for bed, Biscuit!

Woof, woof!

Biscuit wants his doll.

Time for bed, Biscuit!

Woof, woof!

Biscuit wants a hug.

Time for bed, Biscuit!

Woof, woof!

Biscuit wants a kiss.

Time for bed, Biscuit!

Woof, woof!

Biscuit wants a light on.

23

Woof!

Biscuit wants to be tucked in.

Woof!

Biscuit wants one more kiss.

Woof!

Biscuit wants one more hug.

Woof!

Biscuit wants to curl up.

Sleepy puppy.

Good night, Biscuit.

Biscuit, who will you play with today?

Biscuit
Finds a Friend

For two very special friends,
Margaret Jean O'Conner and Willie Hornick.

Woof! Woof!

What has Biscuit found?

Is it a ball?

Woof!

Is it a bone?
Woof!

Quack!

It is a little duck.

The little duck is lost.

Woof! Woof!

We will bring
the little duck
back to the pond.

Woof! Woof!

Here, little duck.

Here is the pond.

Here are your mother
and your father.
Quack!

Here are your brothers
and your sisters.
Quack! Quack!

The ducks say thank you.
Thank you for finding
the little duck.

Quack!
The little duck
wants to play.

Quack!
Woof!

Quack!
Woof!

Splash!

Biscuit fell into the pond!

Silly Biscuit.

You are all wet!

Woof!

Oh no, Biscuit.

Not a big shake!

Woof!

Time to go home, Biscuit.

Quack! Quack!

Say good-bye, Biscuit.

Woof! Woof!

Good-bye, little duck.

Biscuit has found

a new friend.

Silly Biscuit, don't go in the mud!

Bathtime for Biscuit

This one is for my parents.
—A. S. C.

To Sri K.
—P. S.

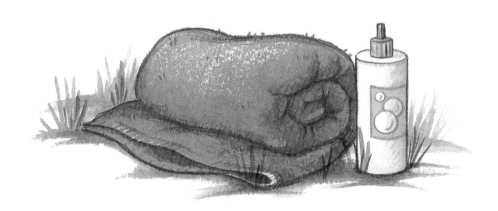

Time for a bath, Biscuit!

Woof, woof!

Biscuit wants to play.

Time for a bath, Biscuit!

Woof, woof!

Biscuit wants to dig.

Time for a bath, Biscuit!

Woof, woof!

Biscuit wants to roll.

Time for a bath, Biscuit!
Time to get nice and clean.
Woof, woof!

In you go!

Woof!

Biscuit does not want a bath!

Bow wow!
Biscuit sees
his friend Puddles.

Woof, woof!

Biscuit wants to climb out.

Come back, Biscuit!

Woof!

Come back, Puddles!

Bow wow!

Biscuit and Puddles
want to play
in the sprinkler.

74

Biscuit and Puddles
want to dig
in the mud.

Biscuit and Puddles
want to roll
in the flower bed.

Now I have you!

Woof, woof!

Let go of the towel,

Biscuit!

Bow wow!
Let go of the towel,
Puddles!

Silly puppies!

Let go!

Woof, woof!
Bow wow!

Oh!

Time for a bath, Biscuit!

Woof, woof!

A bath for all of us!

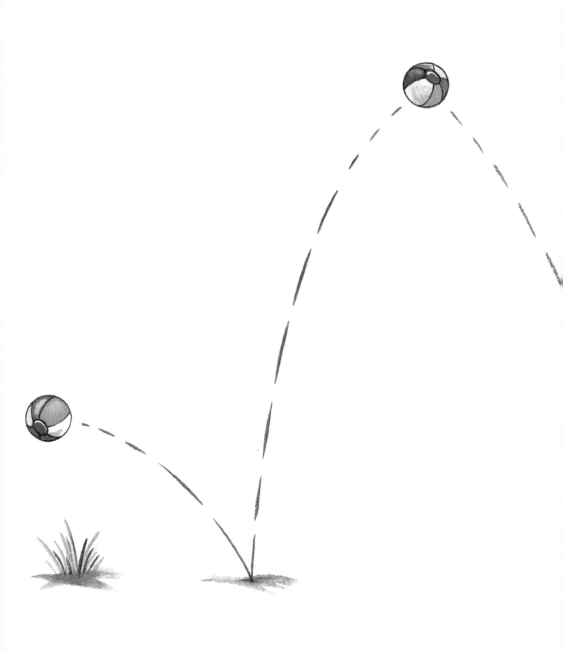

Do you want to learn a trick, Biscuit?

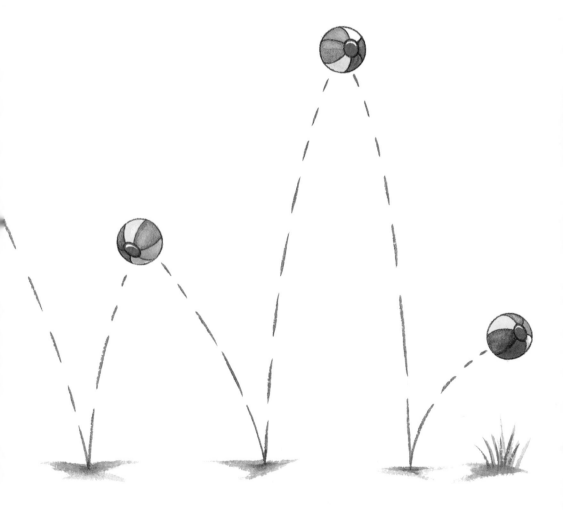

Biscuit's New Trick

For Anthony and Ruby, the newest
–A. S. C.

To Laura
–P. S.

Here, Biscuit!
Look what I have.
Woof, woof!

It's time to learn
a new trick, Biscuit.
Woof, woof!

It's time to learn
to fetch the ball.
Ready?

Fetch the ball, Biscuit.

Woof, woof!

Silly puppy!

Don't roll over now.

Get the ball, Biscuit.

Fetch the ball, Biscuit.

Woof, woof!

Where are you going,
Biscuit?
Woof!

Funny puppy!
Fetch the ball,
not your bone.

Let's try again.

Fetch the ball, Biscuit!

Woof, woof!

Good puppy!
You got the ball.
Woof!

Wait, Biscuit.

Bring the ball back!

Woof, woof!

Let's try one more time.

Fetch the ball, Biscuit!

Woof, woof!

Oh no!
Not in the mud!

Stop, Biscuit!
Don't fetch it now!
Woof!

Oh, Biscuit!

111

You did it!

You learned a new trick!

Woof, woof!

Biscuit, what's that noise?

Biscuit Wants to Play

For Peter, Laura, and Billy
with love
–A. S. C.

Woof, woof!
What's in the basket,
Biscuit?

Meow.

It's Daisy!

Meow. Meow.

Daisy has two kittens.

Woof, woof!
Biscuit wants to play
with the kittens.

Meow. Meow.

The kittens want to play

with a leaf.

Woof, woof!

Biscuit wants to play, too.

Woof!

Biscuit sees his ball.

Meow. Meow.

The kittens see a cricket.

Woof, woof!

Biscuit wants to play, too!

Meow. Meow.

The kittens see a butterfly.

Meow. Meow.

The kittens run.

The kittens jump.

Meow! Meow!
The kittens are stuck
in the tree!

Woof!
Biscuit sees
the kittens.

Woof, woof, woof!

Biscuit can help the kittens!

Woof, woof!

Biscuit wants to play
with the kittens.

139

Meow! Meow!
The kittens want to play
with Biscuit, too!

Woof, woof! Good-bye Biscuit!